ethan's
secret

BY LORIEDITH SERRANO

ILLUSTRATED BY JASON VELAZQUEZ

Printed in the United States of America.
ISBN-13: 978-1-7347356-8-0

Serrano Publishing
New York, NY

To my greatest joy, my beautiful son Ethan. May this pave the way for you to achieve all your greatest dreams. My husband Luis for being my biggest supporter and my greatest friend. My Mami and papi for teaching me to reach for the sky so that if I miss I can land on a star. My family for always believing in me to be great. My niece Destiny who is a real life hero and warrior princess. My best friend Mayleen for sticking in my corner no matter how the seasons change. My Goddaughter Lashay for helping me see my dream into a reality.

And to all you superhero's all around the world, thank you for making dreams come true!

Hi, I'm Catalina. I love to learn new things and teach them as well. This is my friend Ethan, he's four just like me. Ethan is going to be a big brother.

Yesterday Ethan told me the baby is coming really soon but first, they need to have a baby shower.

I wonder why his mom would want to shower babies? That doesn't make much sense at all.

Maybe she wants all the babies to be extra clean before her baby comes, so they won't spread their germs and stuff.

At the shower, I noticed Ethan's mommy didn't have a belly like other mommies do. That's odd don't you think? Where could the baby be growing?

I asked Ethan about his mommy's belly. He said that his mommy was never able to have a baby in her belly. "But how were you born?" I asked Ethan.

Ethan replied, "It's a secret, promise not to tell". "I won't tell, I promise", I said.

"Okay so my mommy knows a superhero, a really nice lady named Destiny." Ethan whispered.

8

"Whoa, that is so cool Ethan!" I shrieked. "Yep. Mommy says Destiny has superpowers-she can carry all types of babies, Destiny's superhero name is Surrogate," Ethan whispered.

"Surrogate? What is that?" I asked quite
confused. "A surrogate is a superhero that
holds the baby in her belly so mommies and
daddies could have babies of their own."

"Mommy says Destiny's superpowers brought them their favorite gift in the world and that's me!" Ethan fist pumped his hand in the air.

"Wow, that sounds awesome." I said excitedly. Ethan looked around to see if anyone was listening. Then he leaned in closer, "Mommy, Daddy and Destiny have secret meetings at the doctor's office. They work really hard to make sure that the baby is a perfect blend of mommy and daddy."

"Look at me, I have my mommy's curly hair and my daddy's eyes." Ethan said happily.
"Oh yes. I can see it, Ethan!"

"Destiny sounds like a really nice lady, I've always wanted to meet a superhero!" I said excitedly.

"Well come on." said Ethan, "She's right over there!"

Anxiously, I waited to see a real-life superhero. There she was, The Amazing...

D-E-S-T-I-N-Y

She wore a cape and a crown just like wonder woman. I could never ever tell Ethan's secret. Destiny was the coolest superhero I have ever met.

CPSIA information can be obtained
at www.ICGtesting.com
Printed in the USA
BVHW021820220620
582089BV00019B/74